The

Well

The Well

GARE CREW • NARELLE OLIVER

FRANKLIN WATTS
NEW YORK • LONDON • SYDNEY

This edition published in 1999 by
Franklin Watts
96 Leonard Street
London EC2A 4XD

Published 1996 by
Thomas C. Lothian Pty Ltd, Australia

Series Editor: Gary Crew

A CIP catalogue record for this book
is available from the British Library.

ISBN 0 7496 3521 5

Printed in Guernsey

Contents

Chapter **One**   7

Chapter **Two**   11

Chapter **Three**   18

Chapter **Four**   23

Chapter **Five**   24

Chapter **Six**   30

Chapter **Seven**   33

Chapter **Eight**   34

Chapter **Nine**   39

Chapter **Ten**   47

Chapter **One**

High in her house on the hill Mrs Ballantyne sat by her fire, watching her grandsons. They were identical twins and knelt at either end of the hearth rug like a pair of fireside dogs. Silent messages were being passed from boy to boy, she knew. She'd had twins herself, once.

'What?' she prompted. 'Tell me. What is it?'

Adam glanced up and smiled. Seth turned to

the fire. Neither spoke.

'Have it your own way,' she said, 'but you're going to bed soon. Believe me, when your mother brings your little brother home, you'll need all the sleep you can get.' She took a sip of tea, and waited.

The boys were the children of her son, Charlie. Their mother was still resting in hospital after the birth of their brother, three days before, so Charlie had brought the twins up to stay.

'Two minutes,' their grandmother warned. 'Two minutes and you're off.'

Adam crossed the rug to his brother and said something behind his hand.

'One minute.'

'Grandma, we've got a special request.' He edged towards her.

'I'm right here. And I'm not deaf. Yet.'

The boy glanced at his brother, read nothing in his face, and turned back to her. 'Grandma, Seth won't ask, but tomorrow, since it's our last proper day here, can we go down to the pine forest? Just for a ...'

'No!' She said this so vehemently that she

surprised herself. She felt her teacup shake. She put it to one side and stood up. 'Bed. That's where you can go. Right now.'

There was a hurried whisper from the mat, and Adam tried again. 'But Grandma, Dad and Mum let us go wherever we like. We're nearly twelve years old. We're allowed.'

'That's at home. Here you're my responsibility.' She picked up the teacup. 'Now go to bed,' and she leaned forward for them to kiss her as they passed.

Adam was put out, she could tell, but he kissed her warmly. Seth's face showed nothing, and when his lips brushed her cheek she shuddered.

Chapter **Two**

The next morning, Mrs Ballantyne took the twins with her when she went shopping in the town. 'If I leave you,' she explained, 'and anything happens ...'

She was a big woman, dark-haired, tall and imposing. Dressed as she was in steely grey, she moved through the shoppers like a battleship, like an ancient iron-clad dreadnought, the crowds parting before her.

The boys wandered along behind, hands in their pockets, shooting glances at each other.

At the butcher's shop, while she fussed over making her choice, the boys stood away, their backs pressed against the wall.

The butcher took the chops she had chosen from the display, wrapped them in white paper and handed them over the counter. He said nothing until he saw the boys.

'They Charlie's kids?' he asked, staring.

Adam smiled. Seth looked down at his feet.

'Yes,' she answered, as if it were none of his business.

'Funny, seeing two of them again. The twins, like ...'

Mrs Ballantyne all but snatched her change from his bloody hand, then motioned for the boys to follow.

At the fruit shop the same thing happened. When the proprietor noticed the boys and asked after them, their grandmother left. At the supermarket, though the check-out girl's questions were perfectly polite, the old woman refused to reply. At the wool shop, where she bought wool to knit booties for the new baby, she was downright rude.

But the incident at the Palms Café was the strangest of all and one which Adam was unable to forget.

They had left the wool shop – Mrs Ballantyne surging on ahead, her shopping bags swinging as she cleared the crowds – when Adam noticed that Seth was no longer beside him. He turned and looked back. He couldn't see his brother behind him either, as no sooner had their grandmother passed through, than the crowds closed up again, a mass of bodies too tall, too thick for a boy to see over or between. He stood still, confused. To go on meant that his brother may be lost; to turn back – to leave his grandma – meant that he may be lost himself, and end up in trouble if she were forced to come looking. All because of Seth. His brother always had to go his own way. Silently. Selfishly. And now, as usual, it was up to Adam to do something. Something *sensible*. Something *reasonable*.

With one hopeless glance back he turned and ran after his grandmother. 'Grandma,' he called, elbowing through the quickly closing crowd. 'Grandma, wait. We've lost Seth.'

'Lost him? How?' And she glared down at Adam as if it were his fault. As if he were his brother's keeper.

The boy shook his head. 'I don't know. One minute he was there, and the next he was gone. He was there when we left the wool shop, I know that, and when we took a quick look in the café, but then ...'

'The café?' she repeated. 'What café?'

'The one near the wool shop. The old one.'

'The Palms,' she muttered, her face suddenly pale. 'The Palms Café,' and she pushed past him, heading back, parting the crowd as she went.

It was dark and quiet inside the café. The waitress at the front counter smiled and attempted to speak, seeming to recognise them, but the old woman did not stop. She strode between the dim, high-backed cubicles where silent couples sat sipping coffee. Not once did she hesitate, nor turn her head to see who she might be passing. It was as if she knew exactly where she was going; as if she knew exactly where her grandson would be seated. When she reached the very last cubicle, to the left, there he was, bending over a tall glass sucking up the frothing dregs of a milkshake.

Sensing her presence, he pushed the glass away and glanced up. His face showed neither surprise nor remorse. 'What?' he said simply.

Still holding her bags, she stared down at him. Adam stood behind her, peeping around. 'What are you doing here?' she demanded.

'I was thirsty,' he answered, almost innocently.

'So you just took it on yourself to come in here. Is that right?'

He said nothing.

'And was that a chocolate milkshake?' she asked.

He nodded.

'Did you pay for it?'

He shook his head. 'That waitress down the front counter gave it to me.'

'*Gave* it to you?'

He looked up at her, his cold, pale eyes meeting hers. 'I never asked for it. As soon as she saw me she told me to take a seat and next thing she came up with this. "On the house," she said. "Like old times." That's what she said. Like she knew me. Or thought I was someone else ...' Then he noticed Adam, standing behind. 'Too bad you missed out,' he said. 'It was nice. Really nice,' and he gave his brother a self-satisfied smile.

'We're leaving,' their grandmother said. She turned and made her way back between the cubicles, fully expecting that the twins would follow – which they did, Adam immediately behind, Seth in the rear. When she reached the front counter, she stepped aside, motioning for them to go through. 'Wait for me outside,' she said. 'I'll pay for that milkshake.'

'The waitress said it was free,' Seth muttered.

'And I said I'd pay for it,' his grandmother replied.

That was the end of the incident, and though Adam pressed his brother for explanations – for some kind of answer – he would never receive one, which was not unusual in dealings with Seth.

But stranger yet, not once throughout that long morning did the grandmother introduce her grandsons. Not once, no matter how often she was asked, did she acknowledge that they existed.

Chapter **Three**

Seth lagged behind as they made their way up the hill to the house. Adam stayed with his grandmother, hurrying to keep up with her in spite of the slope.

'Grandma,' he said, 'how come they all looked at us? How come you ...' But the old woman only increased her stride, leaving the boy to drop back with his brother.

When they reached the house, she unpacked the groceries and made sandwiches. From a cupboard beneath the stairs she produced an old, handmade cricket bat and a moth-eaten tennis ball, its bounce long gone. She sent the boys out to play with them in the back garden.

While they played – one bowling, the other hitting away in spiritless style – she sat on the porch, looking across the grounds, remembering.

She had come here as a bride. A city girl, she'd been, secretary to the director of a mine. When they married, he brought her to this house, and she had gasped at its grandeur. But over the years, since his death, it was the grounds that she had grown to love, their broad expanse sweeping away down the hill towards the distant town.

Beyond the fenced garden, a gravel driveway divided her land into two distinct halves: to her right was the orchard, its trees just breaking into early spring bud; to her left, the pine forest – a good way to make money when it matured, her husband had said – brooding, silvery-green in neglect.

The old woman sighed and got up. 'Coming up

that hill has worn me out. I'm going in for a rest. Stay in the yard, do you hear? We can pick some peas for dinner later. And Seth, give your brother the bat for once.'

The boys played half-heartedly for a while, then sprawled on the grass. From time to time, one rolled on his back to look at the sky.

As usual it was Adam who broke the silence. 'See this?' he asked, holding the bat out to his brother. 'Someone's burnt their name into it. With a magnifying glass, I reckon. It says "Tom", see?'

Seth examined the bat, then wandered off with it among the rows of vegetables, using it to slash at the peas as he went.

Adam followed, gathering the scattered pods and popping the sweet green peas into his mouth. When he reached the end of the row of trellises, there was Seth, leaning on the fence, staring out across the grounds towards the forest.

'We can't go down there,' Adam whispered. 'You heard what Grandma said.'

Seth laughed. He tossed the bat among the peas and leapt over the fence.

Chapter **Four**

Mrs Ballantyne dozed fitfully, long-forgotten images flickering through her brain.

Once, in her dreaming, she saw her husband as a bridegroom. He was young and handsome, dressed in the grey morning suit he had worn at their wedding.

Once, she saw his body crushed beneath the blood-soaked rubble of a mine shaft.

Once, her twin sons beside her, one in tears, the other silent and stony-faced, she saw his open coffin.

Chapter **Five**

As soon as the boys entered the forest, the mid-afternoon sun was swallowed up in shadow. A carpet of pine needles, thick and green, cushioned their footsteps. Silence hung among the trees.

Adam walked hesitantly. He did not want to be there. There was something about the place, something eerie. He looked for the patches of sun and tried to stay in them; he turned constantly, sensing someone behind him – his grandmother maybe, come to get them – but he knew there was no one.

Seth could not have been more different. He dodged between the trees, climbing partway up their trunks then jumping down; he sprang out at his brother, spooking him, only to do the same thing a minute later. Without a care for his grandmother's wishes, he moved deeper into the gloom.

Adam followed, protesting and afraid, yet still his brother ran on, careless, until he reached a clearing among the trees where he suddenly stopped, and stood rigid, staring.

He's tricking me, Adam thought. He's pretending he's seen something. 'Stop fooling around,' he demanded.

Without a word, Seth raised his hand and pointed.

In the centre of the clearing was a stone well. Its roof had long since decayed, but a rusted chain still hung from its handle, disappearing out of sight into the unknown depths of the earth itself.

'So?' Adam said. 'It's just a well. Just a stupid

old well. Come on, let's get out of here. Grandma will be awake and we'll be in trouble. Don't think she's forgotten what happened at the café this morning.' At this he turned, hoping that for once Seth would follow.

He did not. He was moving closer to the well. Slowly, very slowly, approaching from the left he began to circle it, putting it between himself and his twin.

'Come on,' Adam called from the edge of the clearing.

His brother ignored him. Slowly, even cautiously, Seth continued his circling of the well.

'Seth, think of Grandma. Come on. Just for once.'

Still he circled, growing closer with every footstep. His face pale. His eyes wide.

'Seth! This is the last time. The last time ...' But Adam knew his brother would not come. Would not follow. Ultimatums meant nothing to him. Consequences meant nothing to him. Nor threats, nor warnings. Seth had always been the same. So unreasonable, so selfish. And so silent.

Adam folded his arms in a gesture of determination. 'OK then. I'll go back by myself. Seth, do you hear me? I'm going back to the house by myself. I'm going right now.'

But he did not. He stayed where he was, sitting down at the base of a pine to wait. To wait for Seth. And to watch. As he always did.

Not that Seth cared. His senses were focused on the well, on the strange effect that it had upon him. As if it were calling him, beckoning him to come closer.

Soundlessly, his footsteps hushed by the cushioning mulch, he drew near to the edge. Carefully, his thin white fingers extended, he reached out to touch the stone. It was cold. Cold and moist. He trembled, feeling the thrill of that cold run through him. Exciting him. Strengthening him.

He leaned forward, peering into the dark.

'Seth!' He heard his brother's warning call. He leaned further forward, rocking on his stomach, balancing on that cold, stone edge.

'Seth!' he heard again. This time he looked up

and laughed. This time he looked directly at his brother, crouched beneath the distant tree, and laughed outright.

Then he leaned forward once more and, cupping his hands about his mouth, called down into the dark, 'Halloooo ... Is anybody there? Halloooo ...'

Once, he looked up to check whether his brother was afraid.

Once, he reached down to the forest floor and gathered a pine cone. Certain that his brother was watching, he leapt up on to the stone edge and cast it into the depths, calling 'Look out below ...'

Once, he whispered his own name, releasing it like steam. Like a hiss. 'Ssseth ... Ssseth ... Ssseth ...' And each time he turned his head – turned his ear to the mouth of the well – to listen as the word drifted down, as his name drifted down, to be lost in the darkness beneath.

But soon, as always, he grew sick of the game. He gave the dangling chain a good long rattle then began walking back to the house, leaving Adam to run after him, calling for him to slow down. To wait. To say something. To explain.

Chapter **Six**

That night, as the boys sat by the fire, Adam turned to his grandmother and said, 'Grandma, you know that bat you gave to us today, it had the name "Tom" burnt into it. Was he a friend of our Dad's?' The old woman was taken by surprise. 'Tom?' she repeated awkwardly.

'Tom. It was burnt into the bat.'

She put her teacup to one side and smoothed

her skirt. She had known that this would happen, sooner or later. She might ignore the comments of the shopkeepers, the knowing looks of waitresses – of the whole town for that matter – but it couldn't be kept secret forever. Not hidden forever. 'The bat was your uncle's,' she said. 'Your father's brother was called Tom.'

'Dad had a brother?'

'A twin.'

'A twin? Like us?'

'Exactly like you. Twins run in families. It's common.'

'When did he die?'

'Years ago. When he was your age. Almost twelve.'

Seth had said nothing, but now he turned to face her. 'How did he die?' he asked. With his back to the fire, his eyes were twin hollows of darkness.

'He just died, that's all.' She reached out to pick up the teacup, her hand trembling. 'It's bedtime. You had better cover the fire.'

But Seth had not finished. He crept across the rug, almost touching her knees. 'So, why didn't our father tell us?'

'I've already said. It was a long time ago. Maybe he was waiting for the right moment. Maybe he doesn't want to think about it. Like me.' She heard the bitter tone in her voice, and tried to steady herself. 'Besides, this is no time for you to be thinking about that. Your parents will be here in the morning with the baby. Your baby brother. Now there's something to dream about.' And she bent down to be kissed.

Chapter **Seven**

But she was the one who dreamt.

Once, she saw the planting of the pine forest, her husband and her boys working side by side.

Once, she saw them carting water, bucket after bucket, filled from a well.

Once, she saw a boy falling.

Chapter **Eight**

Something caused Adam to wake and sit up. He had no idea what time it was, but the room was dark, the house quiet. What had woken him, he wondered. Why was he so wide awake?

Then he saw his brother seated in the window box, his legs drawn up under his chin, staring out into the night.

'Seth,' he whispered, not wanting to disturb the

old woman. 'Seth, what's wrong?' His brother ignored him.

'Seth,' he repeated, 'what are you looking at?' There was no reply, no sound at all, save for the sigh of a breeze from the garden, the rise and fall of the gossamer curtains.

Throwing back the covers, Adam clambered from his bed and crossed the room to join his brother. He knelt on the window box beside him, glancing first at his pallid face – which told him nothing, as usual – and then at the view from the window.

'What are you looking at?' he asked again. 'I can't see ...' and then he fell suddenly silent, his breath catching in his throat.

In the distance, above the pine forest, a pale green light glowed in the sky. It throbbed like a heartbeat: weak, then strong; weak, then strong, as if it were alive. Or signalling.

'Seth,' Adam whispered. 'What is that? That light ...?'

Still his brother did not reply.

'It's right above the forest. Above that well.

Isn't it?'

Seth laughed. 'Course it isn't. How could it be? There's nothing down there. Maybe it's the lights from the town. Or the sign on that café I was in today. Anyway, who cares?' And with that he swung his legs onto the floor and went back to his bed.

There was something in his brother's voice that Adam did not believe; something in his laugh that he had never heard before. It was forced. False. Uncertain. Which was not like Seth, not like Seth at all, and Adam stayed there, thinking, for a very long time.

When morning came he sat up, shivering. Grey rain trickled down the window. This meant being kept inside, bored to death with ancient board games until their parents came. He glanced over to see if Seth was awake. The bed was empty. He's in the toilet, he thought, or in the kitchen getting his breakfast, and he crawled out to get dressed.

The toilet door was wide open; the kitchen empty. So was the living room – the fire dead. And the yard.

Surely Seth wouldn't be with Grandma, he

reasoned, but he crept back up the stairs to check.

He gently pushed his grandmother's door open and looked in. The room was dim, the curtains still drawn against the night. He saw the mirrored dresser, the looming wardrobe, the teeth in their glass by the bed, and the old woman herself, buried among her pillows, her gummy mouth wide open, her eyelids twitching in dream.

He closed the door without a sound and checked the other rooms, rooms that had been unused for years. He went back to the kitchen. Still no one. He lifted the trapdoor to the cellar and called his brother's name into the dark beneath. There was no answer, nor any hint of movement. Uneasy now, he returned to the bedroom, and there, protruding from beneath the bed, were Seth's crumpled pyjamas. His shoes were missing. And his jeans. And his coat. Then Adam knew where his brother had gone. 'To the forest,' he whispered. 'To that well ...' And in minutes he was running down the hill, cold rain beating against his face.

Chapter **Nine**

Adam made his way through the pines, stopping only when he reached the edge of the clearing. Sure enough Seth was there, standing stock-still in front of the well. His head was uncovered, his hair matted, his coat soaking wet.

'What are you doing?' Adam called, approaching him. 'Why did you come down here?' When Seth turned to him, raising a finger to his lips to demand silence, Adam looked about, expecting something to appear. A forest creature maybe. An animal. Or a bird.

There was nothing.

'What is it?' he whispered. 'What's here?'

Seth smiled his thin smile. His eyes were alive with light, the eerie grey-green of the pines. 'He's here,' he said.

Adam looked about again. 'Who's here?'

'Tom. Our Uncle Tom.'

'Crikey, Seth ...'

'You don't believe me?'

'Course I don't. Grandma said he's been dead for years.'

'But he died right here. Threw himself down the well when his daddy died. Threw himself down, to be with him, in the dark.'

Adam felt the hair rise on the back of his neck. His brother was serious. 'How do you know that?' he demanded, trying to stay in control. 'Grandma didn't tell us that ...'

His brother smiled again. 'Grandma didn't tell us lots of things. She hated Tom. It was our dad

who was her favourite. Her Charlie. So when old Grandpa died, buried in that mine, Tom came down here and threw himself ...'

Adam laughed. 'Crikey, you make stuff up. Half the time you say nothing, and when you do it's all garbage. Do you think you're scaring me, is that it? Like yesterday?'

Seth's smile vanished. His face was stony, his eyes brilliant. 'You want to ask him yourself? You want to ask Uncle Tom yourself?'

Adam shook his head, disbelieving. How come he was always caught out by his brother's stupid games? But as he went to leave, Seth gripped his arm and held him.

'Just wait,' he hissed. 'And watch.'

He released his hold on Adam and moved towards the well. When he reached it, he dropped to his knees and spread his arms wide, resting them on the stone edge. He leaned forward, turned once to check that Adam was watching, then called down into the dark, 'Tom ... Tom, it's me, Seth. I've brought my brother to play. My twin ...'

On that word, a vapour rose from the depths, a

42

curious grey-green vapour, like mist, like smoke, hanging in the throat of the well. It was formless at first, drifting on air, but as Adam watched it took shape: here an arm, there a leg, a lank hand, a bare foot, a grubby shirt, its drooping sleeves flapping loose at the wrist, a pair of tattered trousers rolled at the knee ... and then a head, its pale hair wet and matted ... and then a face, or the ghost of a face, its cheekbones sunken, its mouth thin-lipped, its eyes wan and colourless, sunk deep in hollow sockets that had never seen sun.

Adam shrank back. This thing was himself, the image of himself – and his brother. His twin. Their twin-selves as one. In one ... but one what? *What was this thing?*

Terrified, he covered his mouth, stifling his cry, but Seth lifted his head and called again, 'Tom. Tom.'

On hearing its name the ghost rose higher. It hung on air a moment longer, then sliding to the left, lowered itself to the edge of the well. It looked down on Seth – a cold and calculating look – and turning its back on him, executed a circuit of the stones, walking high upon the balls of its ghastly pale feet, like a dancer, like an acrobat, its arms extended. When it was once again in front of the boys, it bowed low, then stood erect, grinning and cocking its hideous head as if to say, *See what I did? Congratulate me.*

Seth knelt, entranced, his face alive with light. With pale green light.

The thing rose up again, hovered a moment, then looped in the air. Loop after loop, higher and higher, until it all but vanished into the mist that hung in the treetops. It swooped down, diving headfirst into the depths of the well. It remained there long enough to suggest that it had gone, then shot up to the treetops again, laughing as it went. Then it landed again, gentle as a breath, directly before Seth. It leaned forward, reaching out one bony hand. Beckoning. Insistent. It opened its mouth and moved its lips – speaking words that Adam could not hear, murmuring promises he could barely imagine – until Seth took the hand in his, allowing it to lift him up, up onto the edge of the well.

'Seth! Seth, you'll ...' Adam's voice choked in his throat.

Once, his brother turned to him.

Once, he extended his thin, white hand.

Once, he smiled.

As he did the stone began to crack, began to crumble beneath his weight, and then the thing vanished, leaving the boy holding nothing, leaving him to grasp at air as he teetered on the brink of death.

'No!' Adam screamed, lunging forward. 'No ...' In that instant he was pushed aside, and as he fell back, his grandmother gathered his brother up, caught him in her arms, held him to her heart, crying, 'I did love him. I did love him ...' until she sank to the ground, kissing Seth's hair, his face, his eyes, sobbing all the time.

Chapter **Ten**

When their parents arrived, the twins were on the hearth rug, warming themselves beside the fire.

'So, who wants to hold him first?' their mother asked, holding out the baby. Before she could ask twice, Adam cradled him in his arms.

Their father stood by the window, watching. 'Adam,' he said, 'you're a natural,' and chuckling to himself, he turned to take in the view. His face

clouded when he saw the pine forest, grey-green in the misty rain. 'You know, Mum, it's time that timber was cut. How old is it? Twenty years?'

The old woman left her seat to stand by him. 'More,' she said. 'You were ten when it was planted. The same year your father dug the well.'

Charlie frowned. He glanced towards the twins, then back at his mother.

'They know, Charlie. They know all about him. Everything. Now Adam, give Seth a turn. It's his brother too.'

Seth took the baby and held him close. 'Tom,' he whispered. 'That's a good name. I knew a boy called Tom. Once ...'

And a tiny hand lifted to brush his cold, wet lips, to touch the tip of his stony tongue.

AFTER DARK

For details of other chilling
After Dark stories,
read on...

1

The Bent-Back Bridge

by Gary Crew

"The bus rattled across a wooden bridge and turned off the road. Janet looked up from her book. *Is this it?* she wondered, and cupped her hands against the window to peer into the night. The bus had stopped in a clearing among the roadside bushes, but through the darkness she could make out the yellow glow of a telephone box. *There it is*, she said to herself, *like Lola said.*
The driver cut the engine and pushed the cap back from his forehead. 'Here we are,' he called without turning. 'Last stop!'

Then with a suddenness that made her wince, a silver lever shot forward and the door burst open. Janet stepped out into the night..."

Janet has no friends. No friends at all. So when Lola, the new girl in her class asks to meet her at the Bent-Back Bridge after dark, she agrees. Janet would give anything to have a friend... well, almost anything...

2

The Barn

by Gary Crew

"Carter sighed and turned to the window, resting his chin on his hands. 'No,' he said out loud, '*awful* isn't the word for this place,' but as he looked, contemplating a means of escape, a flock of birds flew low over the swamp. In perfect formation, they were shaped like a V. Like an arrow. *Like a sign.* Then, suddenly, gracefully, they arced down to land directly beside the barn.

Hmmm, Carter thought. *Why not?* And pulling on his leather jacket which he wore everywhere to prove that he was still a cool city kid, he tip-toed down the stairs, heading in the direction of the barn..."

Carter Lawrance is cool. He's a city kid. His parents have just bought a run-down farm in the middle of nowhere, and Carter is not happy. Then he discovers the rotting barn in the swamp... and the giant, white worms... and the claw prints of the creature that feeds on them...

AFTER DARK

4

The Crow
by Peter Lawrance

"The vehicle seemed to be accelerating towards them, then the wheels locked as the driver applied the brakes. Travis grabbed Amy and jumped back as it skidded across the road and screeched to a stop.

A face peered from the driver's window. Even in the predawn darkness, Travis felt that the eyes could see all the way into him. The spell was broken by a deep, urgent voice... 'Where's this road go?'..."

Two thieves on the run in a beaten-up van stop to ask thirteen-year-old Travis directions, and his life suddenly shifts gear. On the woman's face is a sinister tattoo, an incarnation of evil. What does it mean, and why does a crow keep appearing out of the empty sky like a dark omen?

Other books in the *After Dark* series

1 **The Bent-Back Bridge**
by Gary Crew and Gregory Rogers

2 **The Barn**
by Gary Crew and Tom Jellett

3 **The Well**
by Gary Crew and Narelle Oliver

4 **The Crow**
by Peter Lawrance and Tom Jellett

5 **The Stray Cat**
by Steven Paulsen and Shaun Tan

6 **The Giant Spiders**
by Stephen Measday and Mark Wilson

7 **The Mouth**
by Carmel Bird and Anita Mertzlin

8 **The Carriers**
by Jonathan Harlen and Tom Jellett